art by Brent Schoonover
lettering by Justin Stewart

cover design by Wim Bens
cover photo by Nicole Schoonover
cover props supplied by Gordon Smuder

Silent Devil is:
co-founders- The Beranek Brothers
business manager- Boryl Beranek
marketing director- Tony DiGerolamo
consigliere- Bruce Levine
fairy godmother- Lauren Perry
production guru- Thomas Mauer

Astronaut Dad Volume One is copyright © 2007 David Hopkins and Brent Schoonover. No part of this book may be reproduced by any means, except for purposes of review, without written permission from David Hopkins and Brent Schoonover.

Published by Silent Devil, Inc.

Printed in Canada.

First Edition
ISBN: 978-0-9796902-2-8

Dedicated to our dads,
Randy Hopkins and Clark Schoonover

David thanks...
Christian Beranek and Silent Devil Productions for trusting us to tell this story, Nunzio DeFilippis and Christina Weir for your helpful edits and mentorship, my daughter Kennedy (I love you!), Brent Schoonover, Justin Stewart, Wim Bens, April Wenzel, Brock Rizy, Tom Kurzanski, Cal Slayton, Diana Nock, Kristian Donaldson, P.J. Kryfko, A.C. Hall, Rob Osborne, Paul Milligan, Jamar Nicholas, Steven New, Melissa Cassidy, Aaron Nelson, Ian Shaughnessy, Leah Wilson and BenBella Books, Richard Neal, Chris Williams, Barry Fuhrman, Matt Price, Joel Pfannenstiel, Joe Noh, Jeremy Shorr, Brad Bankston, Daniel Miller, Dan Hughes, Shanna Caughey, Bethany Keeler, Sarah Jane Semrad and Catherine Cuellar with La Reunion, Clay Harrison, Sean Jackson, Stefan Halley, Jim Lujan, Jeff Elden, Oliver Tull, Luke Hawkins, Scott Hinze and Fanboy Radio for everyone's encouragement and friendship.

Brent thanks...
David for the great script, Silent Devil for the go ahead, Nunzio and Christina for the great help to make the book as best as possible. Gordon Smuder for the perfect vintage space toys, Wim for the designs, Barb Schulz and Terry Beatty for the encouragement. David Hedgecock and Brent Erwin for teaching me the business side of creating comics. Bryan Deemer and Peter Rios of Comic Geek Speak, John Suintres from Word Balloon, Chris, Sal, and Tom of Around Comics, Brandon Terrell, Mike Norton, Steve Bryant, The Sketchjam Crew, Grant Gould, Scott Schomburg, Zander Cannon, Matt and Renae, Nick Post and everyone at The Source Comics and Games, the fine folks at Tomorrow is Yesterday, Mrs. Miller and David Eckburg, Tom Garrett, Frenchy Lunning, the volunteers of the MNCBA, Brett and Nick, Vic, Alice and Clark Schoonover for encouraging creativity, and of course Nicole, for understanding and encouraging me.
I love you.

Chapter One. August 1963.
          The Fall-Out Party.

Chapter Two. November 1963.
Smoking Lessons.

Chapter Three. December 1963.
 The Evening Ride.

CONTINUED IN BOOK TWO

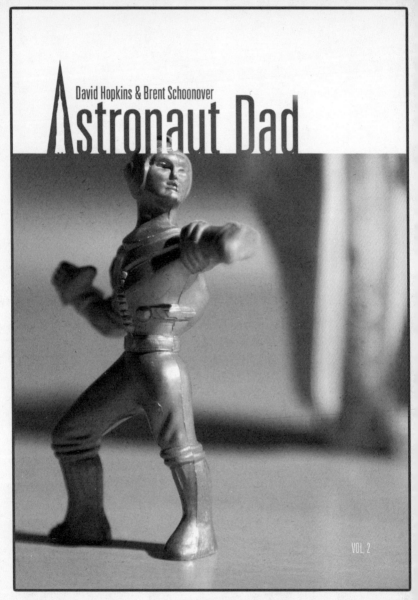